Devil Boys from Beyond

by Buddy Thomas and Kenneth Elliott

Based on an original script by Buddy Thomas

A SAMUEL FRENCH ACTING EDITION

NEW YORK HOLLYWOOD LONDON TORONTO

SAMUELFRENCH.COM

ISBN 978-0-573-69713-5   Printed in U.S.A.   #29123

MUSIC USE NOTE

Licensees are solely responsible for obtaining formal written permission from copyright owners to use copyrighted music in the performance of this play and are strongly cautioned to do so. If no such permission is obtained by the licensee, then the licensee must use only original music that the licensee owns and controls. Licensees are solely responsible and liable for all music clearances and shall indemnify the copyright owners of the play and their licensing agent, Samuel French, Inc., against any costs, expenses, losses and liabilities arising from the use of music by licensees.

IMPORTANT BILLING AND CREDIT
REQUIREMENTS

All producers of *DEVIL BOYS FROM BEYOND must* give credit to the Author of the Play in all programs distributed in connection with performances of the Play, and in all instances in which the title of the Play appears for the purposes of advertising, publicizing or otherwise exploiting the Play and/or a production. The name of the Author *must* appear on a separate line on which no other name appears, immediately following the title and *must* appear in size of type not less than fifty percent of the size of the title type.

A CD containing sound design and music underscoring from the original NYC production is available for licensed productions. The CD also includes accompaniment to the original song, "Sensitive Girl", music and lyrics by Drew Fornarola. Available for licensed productions only, additional music licensing fee will apply. Please contact Samuel French, Inc. for details.

The following required credit shall be given in all programs, posters and publicity material distributed in connection with the performance of the piece:

Sound design and original score by Drew Fornarola
Original sound producer/co-sound design by John Fontein
Original song, "Sensitive Girl", music and lyrics by Drew Fornarola

DEVIL BOYS FROM BEYOND was first produced by MadCap Productions in association with Anna Ashton at the Actors' Playhouse in August 2009 as part of the New York International Fringe Festival, a production of THE PRESENT COMPANY. The performance was directed by Kenneth Elliott, with sets by Brian T. Whitehill, costumes by Gail Baldoni, orginal music, sound design and song by Drew Fornarola, and lighting design by Vivien Leone. The production stage manager was Matthew Karr and the sound producer/co-sound designer was John Fontein. The stage hands were Richard Duffy and Matthew Landen. The cast was as follows:

FLORENCE WEXLER	Everett Quinton
DOTTIE PRIMROSE	Andy Halliday
MATTIE VAN BUREN	Paul Pecorino
GREGORY GRAHAM	Robert Berliner
LUCINDA MARSH	Chris Dell'Armo
GILBERT WIATT	Peter Cormican
JACK PRIMROSE	Jacques Mitchell
HARRY WEXLER	Jeff Riberdy

DEVIL BOYS FROM BEYOND was subsequently produced by David J. Foster at New World Stages in November 2010. The performance was directed by Kenneth Elliott, with sets by Brian T. Whitehill, costumes by Gail Baldoni, orginal music, sound design and song by Drew Fornarola, wigs and hair by Gerard Kelly, and lighting design by Vivien Leone. The production stage manager was Eileen Arnold. The assistant stage manager was Richard Duffy. The stage hand was Frank Boccia. The cast was as follows:

FLORENCE WEXLER	Everett Quinton
DOTTIE PRIMROSE	Andy Halliday
MATTIE VAN BUREN	Paul Pecorino
GREGORY GRAHAM	Robert Berliner
LUCINDA MARSH	Chris Dell'Armo
GILBERT WIATT	Peter Cormican
JACK PRIMROSE	Jacques Mitchell
HARRY WEXLER	Jeff Riberdy

CHARACTERS

(In order of appearance)

FLORENCE WEXLER – A little Southern woman with a big secret.

GILBERT WIATT – A tough New York City newspaper editor.

GREGORY GRAHAM – Burnt out ace photographer and booze hound.

MATILDA VAN BUREN – Star reporter, and legend in her own mind.

LUCINDA MARSH – A headline chasing Grande dame with a nose for news.

DOTTY PRIMROSE – Ancient proprietor of The Evening Primrose Motor Lodge.

HARRY WEXLER – Florence's husband…or is he?

JACK PRIMROSE – Sheriff of Lizard Lick & Dotty's husband…we think.

SETTING

New York City
Lizard Lick, Florida
& beyond

TIME

One hot summer in 1957

PROLOGUE

(In the blackout we hear the sound of a space ship approaching, then an enormous crash. As the lights come up we see two alien creatures emerge, dazed from the wreckage. The first alien gestures to the second and they exit together.)

(A bright white spotlight rises on **FLORENCE.***)*

FLORENCE. I'm not insane, I tell you. I'm not insane! There's something strange going on in this town. It all started last Saturday night when creatures from another planet crashed their spaceship into Harry's tool shed. You shoulda seen that man's face. He just retiled the roof that afternoon, and now, here was this big silver spaceship stickin' straight outa the middle of it, and hundreds of terra-cotta tiles smashed up all over the yard. Harry didn't care if they were from Neptune or Nevada. He went stompin' out to the back yard, madder than a spitball. I stood right here at this window and screamed for him to get back inside before they shot him with a laser beam. He didn't care. I might as well have been recitin' the yeller pages for all he listened. And then he started yellin' at the top of his lungs. "Who the Hell did they think they were, smashing up his fine new terra-cotta roof, and what the Hell did they think they were doing, flying that barge through a residential area at two in the morning, and who the Hell was gonna pay for all those tiles, and who the Hell was gonna clean up his backyard" and that man must have yelled at those poor suckers for fifteen minutes straight. And they just stood there, as polite as can be, just starin' up at him. Well that's when it happened, dear. All of a sudden the whole backyard lit up like the Fourth of July. Red lights. Green lights. Blue lights. White lights. Flashin' on. Flashin off. I screamed at Harry to hightail it inside before they gave him an anal probe, but that geezer has about as much sense as a concrete wall. And then, ZAP! The light disappeared and everything went back to normal. Except that the little space guys were gone. And so was their space-ship. And the tool shed. And the dog. And Harry. My Harry's gone, gone! *(She bursts into hysterical tears.)* I'm not insane! Something evil has taken possession of the town of Lizard Lick!

(quick blackout)

(Lights up instantly on:)

Scene One

(The Newsroom)

(GIL WIATT, *a hard boiled editor, and* **GREGORY GRAHAM,** *ace photographer.)*

WIATT. You mean to tell me that's all we got?!

GRAHAM. I'm tryin' to explain –

WIATT. And you call yourself a photographer. I need pictures! I need a story! *(into an intercom:)* Get Mattie Van Buren in here!

GRAHAM. I hardly think you need to bring *her* into this.

WIATT. You hardly think because you're soused most of the time, Graham, that's your problem.

GRAHAM. I've been clean for ten days since I got out of Cascade. That shock therapy really did the trick!

WIATT. I hope you've dried out for good this time, but I don't have much hope. Once an alkie, always an alkie. I'm giving you one more chance Graham, but I expect you to deliver this time. And I'm sending you out with Mattie.

GRAHAM. I told you I can't work with her!

WIATT. Mattie Van Buren is the best reporter we've got.

GRAHAM. Mattie Van Buren is a hard-boiled bitch.

WIATT. You didn't feel that way when you were married to her.

GRAHAM. Our marriage was pure unmitigated hell!

(MATTIE VAN BUREN, *star reporter, flies in.)*

MATTIE. I heard that Gregory. But I understand. Gilbert, he only talks that way because I won't let him drink. This man could have been the next Margaret Bourke-White!

GRAHAM. Must you emasculate me in front Gil?

MATTIE. Maggie's a great photographer!

GRAHAM. She's a woman!

MATTIE. Well, I'm a woman – what of it? *(with deep concern)* Darling, you know you have a drinking problem. I still care. Have you frisked him, Gil?

WIATT. Nah, what's the use?

GRAHAM. So I'm not to be trusted, is that it?

MATTIE. *(She pats him down.)* You know their tricks.

GRAHAM. *(to* WIATT*)* You see what I mean!

MATTIE. *(finds a flask in his pant leg secured by a string to his belt)* Aha! What's this?

GRAHAM. *(attempting to feign puzzlement)* I don't know how that got there. I haven't worn these pants in weeks.

MATTIE. Then you won't mind if I take it for safe keeping. *(She puts it in her purse.)* Let me smell your breath.

(hits him in the stomach and smells his breath)

MATTIE. He's clean.

WIATT. Now listen you two! I sent you down to Lizard Lick, Florida for a story, a STORY, not this stinkin' drivel about some old bastard blown up in a tool shed!

GRAHAM. Mr. Wiatt, you don't understand –

MATTIE. Oh, clam up Gregory, of course he doesn't understand. This overgrown monkey calls himself an editor, but he can barely speak the English language –

WIATT. Now, Mattie, I'm warnin' you –

MATTIE. Don't warn me, Gilbert, I've got offers from every rag in this country! You don't like my style, I'll cross the street so fast it'll make your head spin –

WIATT. You ain't goin' nowhere, little lady, I'm the only editor in town who'll put up with you!

MATTIE. They'll put up with me, all right, when I flash them my Pulitzer!

GREGORY. That isn't the only thing she'll be flashin'.

MATTIE. That's right, Gregory, dear, I'm up for the Peabody this year, or haven't you heard? *(sympathetically)* I have options, unlike you! I don't burn my bridges, I build them, with the profound power of my poetic pen!

GREGORY. Your pen is as poison as the blood in your veins.

MATTIE. My blood's fine, it's yours that's 80 proof.

WIATT. Can the dramatics and pack your bags. I've booked you both on the nine forty-five.

MATTIE. Splendid, Gil. Where to this time? Budapest? Bombay? The Horn of Africa? I hear the Ivory Coast is absolutely divine this time of year!

WIATT. You're goin' straight back to Lizard Lick and you're gonna find out about these God-damned flying saucers, once and for all!!!

MATTIE. The only thing flyin' in that town is mosquitoes, and I'll be damned if I'm gonna go trudgin' through some bog, tearin' up my nylons!

GRAHAM. We already covered that beat. It's dry!

WIATT. You talked to one old lady!

MATTIE. You're speaking of one Florence Wexler. A simple minded old frump in a house dress babbling about creatures from outer space. Who does she think she is? Orson Welles?

GRAHAM. There's nothin' going on in Lizard Lick, Gil!

MATTIE. And I refuse to be humiliated by pursuing such a puerile and obviously phony story. No, I ain't gonna cover your flying saucers. I wouldn't cover the second coming for you! Even if they held it at the Astor Hotel. I quit!

WIATT. You can't quit without giving notice. I'll sue you!

MATTIE. I certainly can quit. I've got an offer from Henry Luce.

WIATT. Luce! You traitor! Ingrate!

MATTIE. Am I supposed to be grateful for being underpaid?

GRAHAM. Have you got any scotch in the office, Gil?

MATTIE. You see? You're driving him to drink. This is a new low even for you, Wiatt. You've always been a pompous blowhard, but you used to have some integrity. Why would you force me – me! – to cover the lunatic ravings of a desiccated swamp dweller? I'm a reporter, or haven't you figured that out yet?

WIATT. I'm gonna level with you. The newspaper business is on the skids. Mergers, competition from newsreels, radio, and now T.V. It's a rat race. Attention spans are shorter. Nobody's got the time anymore to relax with the evening paper. They'd rather get their news quick from the Camel News Caravan.

MATTIE. Television is not journalism.

WIATT. By the end of 1957 there may only be eight dailies left in New York City.

MATTIE. Oh, Gilbert. I had no idea it was that bad. It's the end of civilization as we know it.

GRAHAM. What's next?

WIATT. Have you every heard of the bread line?! You wanna stand in it? That's what's next! *The Bugle* is this close to going under. I've gotta increase circulation or we'll all be out of a job. I *need* this story! Will you help me?

MATTIE *(after a pause)* I'd like to help you Gil, but I can't pursue a story like this based on a hunch.

WIATT. Does this look like a hunch to you????

(He pulls out a mayonnaise jar with "an alien baby" in it, suspended in a watery solution.)

GRAHAM. *(gasping for breath)* What…what is this-this creature, this demon, this monstrosity-?!?!

WIATT. It's an alien baby, what the hell does it look like, you ninny?!

MATTIE. Oh Gil, put that phony lab specimen away.

WIATT. I thought *somebody* might wanna win herself another Pulitzer, but of course, if *somebody's* not interested, there's always Lucinda Marsh. That broad'd sell her right nipple for a crack at a front page story like this.

*(**LUCINDA MARSH** enters, unbeknownst to the others. She is a headline chasing grande dame with a nose for news, but she has seen better days. She lingers behind them for a moment.)*

MATTIE. You leave Lucinda Marsh of this, you hear me, you baboon??!!

WIATT. What have you got against Lucinda Marsh?

MATTIE. Oh nothing, nothing at all. She gave my name to Joe McCarthy, started a whispering campaign against me at the Ladies Press Club, and told Mamie Eisenhower I was a muff diver.

WIATT. Nobody believes that –

MATTIE. As if that weren't enough, she went on a bender with my drunken husband that ended in our French provincial bed.

GRAHAM. You can't blame Lucinda –

MATTIE. Don't you dare defend her! After what I saw her doing to you in *our* bed – she should be on Ed Sullivan as a contortionist. *(to WIATT)* Why you continue to run her venomous column I'll never understand.

WIATT. She sells papers.

MATTIE. That right-wing cooze isn't a journalist! She's a fetid cesspool of bigotry, lies, and lascivious innuendo. She stinks, you hear? I could smell Lucinda Marsh and her ten cent toilet water *(She sniffs.)* if she were… *(She sniffs again, bigger:)* …if she were five miles away.

(MATTIE whirls around. She is nose to nose with LUCINDA.)

LUCINDA. How bout five inches, dear?

MATTIE. *(Total change in personality. Dripping with fake affection)* Lucinda, darrrling…..wherever did you…*drop* in from?

LUCINDA. Simply slumming, dear. My interview with Audrey Hepburn's been delayed, so I thought I'd see how it goes in *(with icy disgust)* the *newsroom.*

MATTIE. It goes just swell, Lucinda, although I must admit I've suddenly been overcome with the most intense wave of nausea.

LUCINDA. Nausea suits you, dear. It goes with your dress. Whyyyyyy Gregggory. It's been a long time…I haven't seen you since before your nasty, nasty divorce. Pity, that.

WIATT. Listen. Lucinda, we're in a meeting –

LUCINDA. So I see…and what is this little gargoyle? Mattie, dear, mayonnaise jars are no place to preserve your stillborns.

MATTIE. *(charges at her:)* Now listen you home wrecking bitch-!

WIATT. All right, that's enough of that –

LUCINDA. I'll say. Mattie, dear, they have a remedy for that kind of behavior –

MATTIE. I have a remedy for you old lady, hemlock!

WIATT. Lucinda, I'm afraid I'm going to have to ask you to excuse us –

LUCINDA. No need, Gilbert, darling, I've got to fly. But I must say I'm quite intrigued by your little jarhead. Wherever did it come from?

MATTIE. Don't you tell her anything about this story, Gil.

LUCINDA. A *story*! Gilbert! Are you holding out on me?

WIATT. You got nothin' to worry about Lucinda, now if you'll excuse us –

LUCINDA. But of course, I must run. I'm cocktailing it at the Colony with Father Coughlin. He's hoping for a comeback and I'm going to help him. Ta, dears. Hope all goes well with your little jarhead.

(She exits with a sinister look back at the jar.)

MATTIE. I told you to keep her away from me!

WIATT. Forget Lucinda Marsh, you've got a case to crack.

MATTIE. I'd rather crack her skull and watch the marbles roll out.

GRAHAM. Gil, where, where did that jar come from to begin with?

WIATT. That's what you're gonna find out, Einstein! It came from Lizard Lick, Florida, air mail, no return address. Just this note.

*(**MATTIE** snatches it.)*

MATTIE. *(reading)* "They have landed."

GRAHAM. They have landed? Who have landed?

WIATT. It ain't Amelia Earhart, buddy boy.

MATTIE. Gil, I have to be honest with you. I think you've lost your mind. There's no such thing as flying saucers. There are no creatures. That is nothing more than a deformed frog in a mayonnaise jar. It's pure paranoia. But if you think this story will save *The New York Bugle*, I'll take the assignment! New York needs nine daily papers. But remember, you owe me one pal. Let's go Gregory!

WIATT. Wait, your itinerary!

MATTIE. Keep it, ya fat ape, after that last hotel you stuck me in, I'll make my own reservations!

*(She is exiting across the stage, **GRAHAM** chasing her, **WIATT** chasing both of them. He has left the itinerary sitting on top of the alien baby jar.)*

WIATT. But there's only one hotel in Lizard Lick!

MATTIE. Then it looks like I'll be campin' on the beach!!!

*(They all exit, and at the moment they do, **LUCINDA MARSH** appears at the other side of the stage and slinks over to the jar. She picks up the itinerary, her eyes growing wide, and smiles with great cunning, an evil barracuda.)*

(blackout)

Scene Two

(En route to Lizard Lick)

(The inside of the plane to Lizard Lick: a row of five chairs in a line parallel to the front of the stage facing right. **MATTIE VAN BUREN** *is in the first seat. Next to her is* **GREGORY GRAHAM**. *The passenger furthest to the back is reading a large newspaper, which conceals her, totally.)*

MATTIE. Its wonderful to be working together again, Isn't it darling? After we finish this assignment, I think we should take a vacation together, Greg, just the two of us. It'll be like old times. We'll go someplace where nobody knows us, where nobody knows about your "problem."

GRAHAM. Sounds marvelous. The nurse and the invalid. Spare me your infernal solicitude.

MATTIE. I just thought after what you've been through at Cascade –

GRAHAM. Where is the stewardess? If you'll excuse me I'm going to find the little boys room.

(He stands and walks to the back of the plane.)

A WOMAN FROM BEHIND A BIG NEWSPAPER.
     Psssst! ……………………………Pssssst!

*(The woman behind the newspaper throws it down, revealing….***LUCINDA MARSH***!!!)*

GRAHAM. Lucinda! You're supposed to be…you ought to be…I mean you shouldn't be –

LUCINDA. Stop your sputterin' and sit down. I've got our favorite. *(She produces a flask from her purse.)* We'll make it a loving cup.

GRAHAM. *(As he speaks,* **LUCINDA** *is mixing two drinks.)* Can the act, Lucinda. You don't fool me anymore. I'm onto you and your wicked schemes. You slithered into my life like a poisonous snake –

LUCINDA. On the rocks, or straight up?

GRAHAM. Straight up, thanks...You wrecked my career, destroyed my marriage, your heart is cold, Lucinda Marsh!

LUCINDA. *(handing him a drink)* Oh, dear, dear Gregory, always the comedian.

GRAHAM. What the hell are you doing here, Lucinda? If Mattie finds you on this plane –

LUCINDA. But she won't find me, see?!?! I'm travelin' incognito! *(She slaps on a pair of huge dark glasses.)* She'll only find out if you tell her, and you wouldn't sing to the coppers now, would you, Gregory, dear?

GRAHAM. I have no loyalty to Matilda Van Buren anymore. She's so "good." So good she had me locked up in a sanatorium to dry out after she caught you and me in flagrante delicto. I can't tell you how sick I am of being watched all the time. Always suspected of taking a drink. *(He swallows the whiskey in a gulp.)* But you? You're a scorpion!

LUCINDA. Foolish boy. So little you know of the real Lucinda Marsh.

GRAHAM. I know you seduced me and wrecked my marriage!

LUCINDA. Oh, Gregory, I never meant to cause you pain. I only wanted to save you from the fangs of that pinko dyke – *thing* – you called a wife.

GRAHAM. Mattie and I were in love! You were simply jealous of an emotion you could never feel, and of a writer you could never be!

LUCINDA. Lies, all lies!!!!

GRAHAM. You haven't changed, Lucinda. Thanks for the drink.

(He turns to go.)

LUCINDA. But Gregory...I simply *must* speak to you! You haven't even asked me why I'm here!

GRAHAM. I may be drunk but I'm not stupid! You're here to scoop our story!

LUCINDA. *(slyly:)* Story? Why, I don't know what you're talking about, Gregory…unless maybe you're referring to…THIS!!!

(She has yanked the alien baby out of her purse. It is no longer in the watery solution, and it drips with slime.)

GRAHAM. Good God, are you mad, woman?!? What have you done!?!

LUCINDA. *(cackling crazily)* What have I done?! I've found the story that's going to make me the most famous reporter in the world!

GRAHAM. Have you lost your mind?! This vile beast was in a jar, Lucinda!

LUCINDA. That fat jar wouldn't fit in my purse!

GRAHAM. You don't know what you're dealing with! This could be some freak of nature, riddled with disease! Sweet Jesus! You may have exposed this plane, this planet, to a fate worse than death!

LUCINDA. The only fate worse than death is a marriage to Mattie Van Buren, and I already saved you from that!

GRAHAM. Lucinda, for the love of God, put it away! Put it away!

LUCINDA. First you tell me what this is all about, you sniveling lush!

GRAHAM. All right! All right! It's about space ships!

LUCINDA. Space ships?

GRAHAM. Space ships! Flying saucers! Creatures from another world! Mattie doesn't believe it, but I do.

LUCINDA. She didn't believe there were queers working in the State Department either, but I exposed them.

GRAHAM. They're here, Lucinda! They're here, and they've landed in Lizard Lick, Florida!

LUCINDA. Aliens from outer space…how absolutely perfect. It's the scoop of the century, and Lucinda Marsh is going to break it to the world!

GRAHAM. You can't! The story is ours!

LUCINDA. It's mine, you hear!?! Either you're with me or against me!

GRAHAM. What are you suggesting?!?! That I leave Mattie Van Buren and team with you?

LUCINDA. That's precisely what I'm suggesting! An alliance! Lucinda Marsh, star reporter, defender of the American way of life, and Gregory Graham, ace photographer. Together we'll touch the bottom of this treacherous swamp! We'll destroy the aliens and our names will be in history books! Awards will line our walls and cold hard cash will line our pockets! Join me Gregory! Leave Comrade Van Buren and meet your destiny!

GRAHAM. *(considers her for a moment, then)* I'll have to take a rain check on that. Thanks for the drink, Lucinda.

(He starts to walk away.)

LUCINDA. You'll regret this, Gregory. You'll regret the day you chose her over me! I'll break this story, you hear?!? And when I do, you two hacks'll be moppin' up your tears in a greasy diner, cause that's the only place you'll ever work again!!! I'm queen of the blacklist, baby, and you're gonna be on it!

(Blackout. Ominous music. Lightning. Thunder. As the scene changes, we see the plane [a model plane on a string] flying wildly through a treacherous sky.)

(blackout)

Scene Three

(The Evening Primrose Motor Lodge)

*(**DOTTY PRIMROSE**, a very ancient and very faded southern belle, enters, followed by **MATTIE** and **GREGORY**, who is carrying a suitcase.)*

DOTTY. I hope you like this room better. I aired it out, but it don't do much good with suffocating humidity, not a whisper of a breeze, and the swamp cooler on the fritz.

MATTIE. But you say you've seen these aliens?

DOTTY. Oh, I seen 'em, I seen 'em there's no denyin'. Devil boys, I call 'em, devil boys from beyond.

MATTIE. What did they look like, these devil boys?

DOTTY. They were real purty, if you can call a man purty: angel faces, rippling flank muscles, skin as smooth as baby's bottom. That's the way the devil comes, and I've seen the devil. I've had visions. They call me a visionary. Let me get your valise.

GRAHAM. *(the suitcase)* Please, let me help you with that –

DOTTY. Mr. Graham, honey, I wouldn't dream of it. I'm stronger than I look. Why, when I was a girl I used to arm wrestle all my gentleman callers at the Moon Lake Casino. And I always won. *(She attempts to pick up the suitcase.)* I got it...I got it...I got it. *(She drops it.)* I ain't got it. *(She tries again.)* I got it...I got it...I got it. *(She drops it.)* I ain't got it. *(She tries again, and this time she manages to lift it to the luggage rack with great effort.)* I got it...I got it...I got it! *(She gives **GRAHAM** a flirtatious smile.)*

MATTIE. But what do these so called devil boys have to do with Martians? Just sounds to me like a couple of handsome young fellas happened to walk down Main Street. Nothing unusual in that.

DOTTY. Oh, it was unusual, all right, because all the men in Lizard Lick are fat and ugly.

MATTIE. I see. Mrs. Primrose –

DOTTY. Call me Dotty.

MATTIE. Very well…Dotty. Have you noticed any other odd goings-on in town lately?

DOTTY. Odd…? Why everything is odd in Lizard Lick, Miz Van Buren. We are a town that cultivates its eccentricity like an exotic flower.

GRAHAM. You don't understand. What Miss Van Buren means is have you noticed anything out of the ordinary?

DOTTY. Anything ordinary would be out of the ordinary in Lizard Lick, Mr. Graham. Something about the toxic fumes makes daily routine of any kind difficult if not impossible.

MATTIE. I see. Have there been any unnatural occurrences of any kind?

DOTTY. Naturally there have been what you Yankees might call unnatural occurrences. Generation upon generation of inbreeding has made Lizard Lick a center for sexual perversions of the most extreme and unspeakable nature.

MATTIE. Can you elaborate on that?

GRAHAM. Oh, Mattie, she's useless. Can't you see her brain is pancake batter?

DOTTY. Now what's *unusual* is the invasion –

MATTIE. Invasion?

DOTTY. …or should I say migration of all you New Yorkers to our quaint little backwater.

MATTIE. All us New Yorkers? All who? It's just Gregory and me.

DOTTY. It's not just you. Now I got that ol' bleach blonde crone in cottage C.

MATTIE. Bleach – what?!?

DOTTY. Jane Doe, she said her name was.

MATTIE. Lucinda Marsh is in that room! I'll stake my Pulitzer on it!

GRAHAM. Mattie, control yourself!

MATTIE. Mrs. Primrose, you are dismissed. I shall expect hot coffee and scones at seven a.m.

DOTTY. Sure, honey. And I shall expect Rock Hudson ta eat my bald pussy at ten.

(She exits.)

MATTIE. How dare Lucinda follow us down here!

GRAHAM. Well what do you wanna do, Mattie??

MATTIE. *(opening the suitcase to unpack)* I want to stop that bitch dead in her tracks. There must be a story if she's hauled her ass down here. But what is it? Somebody's perpetrating a hoax. But why? Why? *(She discovers a bottle of bourbon in the suitcase.)* Oh Gregory, what's this?

GRAHAM. *(evasively)* I don't know. It looks like a bottle of bourbon.

MATTIE. Yes, that's what it is. How did it get here?

GRAHAM. I have no idea. I told you I haven't touched the stuff for ten days. I'm clean.

MATTIE. You're lying. You reek of the stuff. You were drinking on the plane.

GRAHAM. How could I be drinking? You were sitting right in front of me! You don't trust me.

MATTIE. I wasn't going to say anything, but I saw you knocking 'em back with that old battle axe in the last row.

GRAHAM. Will you stop watching me all the time! That's how you get your kicks. You don't need me. You don't need anyone or anything. You never have.

MATTIE. But you're wrong, Gregory, oh, can't you see how wrong you are? I need, Gregory. Ohhh, how I need.

(He almost gives in to her, then pushes her roughly aside.)

GRAHAM. So do I. I need a drink.

MATTIE. You always chose the bottle over me!

GRAHAM. And you always chose the newsroom over me. What do you care? You're the one who walked out, or don't you recall?

MATTIE. I left you all right, because you broke our sacred marriage vows.

GRAHAM. You know you were always first in my life!

MATTIE. Until you decided to sleep with a corpse!

GRAHAM. So I made a mistake.

MATTIE. Lucinda's old enough to be your mother! Really, Greg, how could you.

GRAHAM. One time! I was seduced!

MATTIE. It makes me sick to think about it.

GRAHAM. You were at the office working late on a deadline as usual, but you made damn sure I wouldn't fall off the wagon that night. Living with you was like being in Sing-Sing.

MATTIE. Let's not go over this again.

GRAHAM. You'd drained every bottle in the house, even the one I hid in the vacuum cleaner. Oh, you were ever so careful. You'd taken my keys, my wallet, and every pair of pants in the house. I was going mad. Then the doorbell rang. It was Lucinda, and she'd brought along her good friend Old Grand Dad.

MATTIE. For a sleazy night with Lucinda Marsh and a bottle of hooch, you threw our love away!

(She glares at him with hatred.)

GRAHAM. Don't look at me like that.

MATTIE. And by the time I got home you had the DTs. You were seeing bats, and rodents, pink elephants, and, oh yes, little green creatures popping up in the window!

GRAHAM. That's all in the past. We're here on business. I'm trying Mattie. I'm trying.

MATTIE. You're trying not to drink, and I'm trying not to love you.

GRAHAM. Do yourself a favor and clear out.

MATTIE. Oh Gregory…what happened to us…once we danced beneath a velvet midnight sky…moonlight in our hair, stars in our eyes, the future at our grasp… it was wonderful! But in the end our love was not enough, my darling.

GRAHAM. Can the dramatics, you're makin' me sick.

MATTIE. Oh, Gregory, we're all alone, you and I, in this cold and desolate town. We may not escape with our lives. Fuck me, Gregory!

(GRAHAM *almost kisses* MATTIE. *Then, suddenly, he pushes her away.*)

GRAHAM. It's too late, Mattie. What we had is through. How did you ever get mixed up with a guy who sops it up like me? I'm a hopeless alcoholic, and all I want is a drink.

MATTIE. And all I want is to make damn sure you don't have one. So if you don't object, I shall pour this down the toilet.

(*She exits with the bottle.*)

GRAHAM. Delighted. Why don't you take my keys and lock me in like a dog while you're at it?

MATTIE. (*offstage*) You'll thank me for this, darling!

(*There is the loud and unmistakable sound of flying saucers outside the window. A hanging light over the bed begins to swing wildly back and forth. The bed begins to shake. The night-stand next to it rattles, and spills everything on top of it across the floor.* GRAHAM *runs to the window. Colored lights have now begun to blink turbulently outside the window.*)

GRAHAM. There's something out there!

MATTIE (*offstage*) Can't hear you!

GRAHAM. (*staring out the window*) Mother of God! It's the size of a football field!

MATTIE. If you're hiding any other bottles, now is the time to fess up!

(*Instantly, a huge disgusting alien pops up right outside the window and roars.* GRAHAM *screams. The flashing lights suddenly cease, as does the rest of the pandemonium, but* GRAHAM *continues to babble.* MATTIE *re-enters.*)

MATTIE. Greg, what's wrong? What's happened

GRAHAM. *(writhing on the floor)* No, don't let them take me, don't let them give me the anal probe—!!! Or the nipple clamps! Or the-or the- hot wax!

(He is writhing in ecstasy, at the thought. He sees **MATTIE** *staring at him. And stops.)*

Well don't give me that look. Everyone knows aliens like to party!

MATTIE. Oh Gregory. Not the DTs again! You *have* been on a toot!

GRAHAM. It was an alien. A Martian. A green creature!

MATTIE. Of course, of course, I know. And pink elephants too.

GRAHAM. I've never seen anything so horrifying, so ugly.

MATTIE *(taking out a funnel)* I'm going to force-feed you a gallon of hot coffee and you'll see that it was all in your imagination. Promise me that you'll never take another drink!

GRAHAM. But it was real, I tell you! Right there! Right There!

MATTIE *(checking the window)* There's nothing there. Just the swamp. Now promise!

GRAHAM. Yes, yes, I promise. But we have to warn Lucinda – she's in danger!

MATTIE. Lucinda?

GRAHAM. We've got to warn her. *(as he exits)* They're here! They're here!

MATTIE. Greg, come back!

*(***MATTIE*** *runs out after him. Blackout.)*

(Loud suspense music blasts up. Quick special up on **MATTIE** *and* **GREGORY** *"running" frantically through the night. Lights fade out on them as they rise on:)*

Scene Four

(Lucinda Marsh's hotel room)

(It is the same room that Mattie and Graham used in the previous scene. Only difference is that this one has Lucinda's luggage.)

*(**LUCINDA** enters from the bathroom in a flowing nightgown.)*

(She begins to get ready for bed, turning down the sheets, putting on face cream, moisturizing her elbows, the whole works. She is humming, in a good mood.)

*(There is a rough knocking at the door, then **GREGORY** enters.)*

GRAHAM. Are you still alive?!? Is it too late?!?

LUCINDA. *(throwing herself into **GRAHAM**'s arms)* Never too late for you. How about a cocktail, big boy?

GRAHAM. *(scoping out the room, frantically)* You mean you haven't seen any Martians? Flying saucers? Blinking lights?

LUCINDA. Blinking lights, of all the nonsense, Gregory, honestly –

GRAHAM. You've been here all night and seen nothing strange?

*(**MATTIE** enters.)*

LUCINDA. Unless you refer to this fungi before me –

MATTIE. My, my, if it isn't Jane Doe in the flesh. Clever alias Lucinda, it's almost as obvious as your writing. I've got a good mind to get on that horn to Gil Wiatt and blow the whistle on you!

LUCINDA. Blow away, dear. That's something you do well. And as far as Gil Wiatt is concerned, I came to this charming countryside for simple rest and relaxation. Lucinda Marsh is overworked, overstressed and needs to get back to basics and find herself.

MATTIE. Tell her to try lookin' in the morgue.

GRAHAM. *(stepping in)* Stop it! Stop it! Enough of this petty squabbling! Can't you two see we've got to put the past behind us and work together?!

LUCINDA. *(brimming with revulsion)* Work together…????

MATTIE. Don't tell her anything! She'll scoop us!

GRAHAM. This is bigger than a scoop! We've no clue what these fiends are after!

MATTIE. There aren't any fiends.

GRAHAM. They may be bent on world domination, or something even *more* sinister! Your prizes and awards will mean *nothing* when you're chained to a wall as an alien's concubine!

MATTIE. Darling, this is the worst I've ever seen you. It's the booze talking, can't you see!

GRAHAM. Get yourself dressed, Lucinda.

LUCINDA. My, my, Gregory, darling. That's the first time you ever asked me to put *on* my clothes, wherever do you think we're going?

GRAHAM. To pay a little visit to Florence Wexler. Somethin's fishy with that broad and it ain't shrimp cocktail.

LUCINDA. You imbeciles leave my room this instant or I'll call the authorities and have you both hauled to the clink!

MATTIE. Come Gregory, it's obvious the bag needs her beauty sleep.

LUCINDA. Ohh, I'm not going to sleep, Nancy Drew. While you fools gallivant through this hick town searching for clues, I'll be lounging in my silk nightie, waiting for the clues to come to me.

MATTIE. You're crazier than a barrel of monkeys.

LUCINDA. Am I?

GRAHAM. Dammit, she's right! I never thought of this! It's brilliance! Pure brilliance!

MATTIE. What is she talking about, Gregory?! Damn you, TELL ME!!!!!!!!

GRAHAM. She's got that alien baby!!!

LUCINDA. Stop blubbering! I put it back in its jar

GRAHAM. She'll use it as bait, and those heinous beasts will fly straight to her doorstep!

LUCINDA. *(pulling out a huge net on a stick)* And when they dare show their mugs, I'll scoop them up in this butterfly net and sell them all to the Bronx Zoo.

MATTIE. How very resourceful of you. Come on, Gregory, let's follow up with Florence Wexler.

LUCINDA. Unless, of course, Gregory would rather stay with me and write love songs??

GRAHAM. I tried to warn you, Lucinda. Now you're on your own.

LUCINDA. What a heartbreak. How will I survive. Just me, myself, and two bottles of bourbon.

*(She whips a bottle out from behind her back. **GRAHAM** is transfixed. Crazy music up.)*

Come on, baby. You know you're a slave to my…jugs.

(She is holding two bottles now, massaging them against her breasts.)

MATTIE. You're out of luck, Bitch! Gregory's off the sauce, or didn't he tell you?!

*(**LUCINDA** is now slinking away, flicking little splashes of bourbon at **GRAHAM**, who follows like a puppy dog.)*

LUCINDA. Ohh, poor, baby boy. Jump off that rickety old wagon. You can take a ride on Lucinda's magic carpet.

(Now she is massaging a bottle lewdly against her pelvis.)

MATTIE. *(horrified)* Gregory! For the love of God! What's come over you?!? You promised me!

LUCINDA. You know you want it. You know you need it. Come on baby!

*(**GRAHAM** is on his knees in front of her. She pours huge streams of bourbon into his mouth.)*

MATTIE. *(hysterical)* You're evil, Lucinda Marsh. You're a cold blooded vampire!

LUCINDA. Just tryin' to quench a man's thirst.

MATTIE. His liver's already the size of a Buick! You were trying to kill him, that's what you were trying to do! Is there nothing you won't stoop to for a story?!?

LUCINDA. *(advancing on them dangerously)* Darlin', you finally hit the nail on the head. There's nothing I won't stoop to for a story. *Nothing, ya hear?!?!* This is my story, see?? I'm gonna crack it see?? And if I get to crack your skull while I'm at it, that'll just be the icing on the cake. So hit the road, shitface! And take this lousy sponge with ya. This town ain't big enough for the three of us!

MATTIE. You're mad!

LUCINDA. *(She cackles hysterically.)* Deliciously!

MATTIE. Come on, Greg!

LUCINDA. Grow some eyes in the back of your head, cunt. You're gonna need 'em!

(And with that, she gives them a giant shove out the door and slams it with all her might. She picks up the jar, opens it, and addresses the "alien baby" inside.)

LUCINDA. If my hunch is correct, your mama and papa will come looking for you, and the story of the century will walk right into my room. You're really quite adorable

(She opens the lid of the jar. She sticks her finger in it.)

LUCINDA. Kootchie kootchie koo!

(Instantly, the creature pops up and roars a blood-curdling roar. LUCINDA screams a blood-curdling scream. But before she can save herself, the creature flings itself onto LUCINDA's face and attaches itself there, ala "Alien." LUCINDA falls back limply onto the bed, the creature hanging there from her face, making eerie sucking sounds. The music is filled with danger.)

(blackout)

Scene Five

(In front of Florence Wexler's house)

(MATTIE runs on, dragging GRAHAM behind her.)

MATTIE. Here we are. Six-twenty-five Oak Tree Lane, and look. There's a light on!

GRAHAM. It's almost midnight, for Godsake Mattie, let's come back tomorrow.

MATTIE. You're the one who wanted to come here in the first place. Now you want go back to the hotel. What's going on? You're working with her, I can sense it in the marrow of my bones!

GRAHAM. Get over it baby, you're the only dame I work with.

(He pulls MATTIE toward him. She's not buying it.)

MATTIE. You're drunk! All a girl's gotta do is flash a bottle and you come runnin'!

GRAHAM. The only girl I'll ever run to's you, Mattie.

MATTIE. *(a million conflicting emotions)* You bastard. A belly full of booze and you toy with my fragile emotions, well you can't, Gregory! I won't let you!

(GRAHAM kisses her neck passionately. MATTIE swoons.)

How dare you! You – you good for nothing – you son of a bitch -you –

(He kisses her with enormous passion. MATTIE gives in. The kiss ends and GRAHAM wraps himself into her arms, puts his head on her shoulder, his eyes closed.)

MATTIE. Oh Gregory....oh darling, can it be true? Have you now at long last realized that our passion is an eternal flame, blazing through the night in the lighthouse of love? Oh Gregory, tell me it's true and we'll leave this wicked place at once! Let Lucinda have her prizes! All I need is you, my darling. You're all I ever needed... Gregory?...Gregory??

GRAHAM. *(snores loudly, passed out cold on her shoulder)*

(The front door of **FLORENCE WEXLER**'s *house flies open and* **FLORENCE** *storms out, in a bright red teddy and giant pumps.)*

FLORENCE. WHAT IN THE HELL IS ALL THE RACKET OUT HERE?!? I'LL HAVE YOU TWO KNOW THIS IS PRIVATE PROPERTY, SO TAKE YOUR SCREECHIN' ASSES AN' GIT!

(GRAHAM *and* **MATIE** *do double takes, confused at* **FLORENCE WEXLER**'s *outfit.)*

MATTIE. *(truly baffled)* …Mrs. Wexler?

FLORENCE. Who wants to know?!

MATTIE. Mrs. Wexler, what on earth are you wearing?! It's positively indecent!

FLORENCE. *(suspiciously)* Wait a minute…I know you… you're them two high falutin' reporters what was buzzin' round here askin' questions last week!

MATTIE. Yes, that's right, and we wonder if you'd mind –

FLORENCE. You bet your mother I'd mind! I got nothin' ta say ta you crackers!

GRAHAM. Mrs. Wexler, this is a matter of national security! The fate of mankind could hang in the balance!

FLORENCE. Fuck mankind!!

GRAHAM. Mrs. Wexler!!!

FLORENCE. Still here, are ya?? I'm warnin' you two, and I don't warn twice!

MATTIE. Mrs. Wexler, what's come over you?! Last week you made us lemonade and sugar cookies, welcomed us into your home with open arms, and tonight you're a hard-boiled bitch!

GRAHAM. If I didn't know any better…

MATTIE. It's almost as though you're a different person altogether!

*(***MATTIE** *and* **GRAHAM** *exchange horrified looks.)*

GRAHAM. Mrs. Wexler, don't you realize we could help you get your husband back?!

FLORENCE. Honey, my husband's back!

GRAHAM. He's *back*?!

MATTIE. But when –

FLORENCE. He's been back, mystery's solved, so high tail it outa here before I –

MATTIE. Oh, but we simply *must* speak to him –

FLORENCE. Outa the question –

MATTIE. We've got to! *(calls inside)* Mr. Wexler! Mr. Wexler, can we speak to you?!

FLORENCE. Are you lookin' for an ass beatin', bitch?!

*(Suddenly, a giant muscle-bound **HUNK** of a man, not older than 30, and clad only in a tiny, tiny shiny red thong appears in the doorway.)*

HUNK. Is there a problem sweetheart?

MATTIE. Oh my goodness!

GRAHAM. I think perhaps we've come at a bad time.

MATTIE. Mrs. Wexler! This is appalling!

GRAHAM. Now, Mattie, we're not here to judge –

MATTIE. I call em as I see em!

FLORENCE. I don't think you understand –

MATTIE. Oh, I understand, all right. What kind of a scam job are you runnin?

FLORENCE. Scam job?!

GRAHAM. Mattie, what on Earth are you trying to pull?!

MATTIE. Oh Gregory, open your eyes! Can't you see?! This isn't about spaceships! *This* is about lust! Greed! And *murder*!

FLORENCE. Murder?!?

MATTIE. Hit a nerve did I, FLORENCE?!? *This* is the kind of story I know how to cover!

FLORENCE. Honey, have you lost your ever lovin' mind? I am an eighty-two year old woman. I can barely peel a banana! How the hell do you think I had enough strength to kill someone!?

MATTIE. Ya had enough strength to squeeze your fat ass into that teddy didn'tcha?!

FLORENCE. Now listen here – !

GRAHAM. …Uh, Mattie, I think maybe we should –

MATTIE. So how'd ya off 'im, Flo? Gunshot? Knife in the back? Maybe a nice clean strangling?!?

FLORENCE. I don't know what you're talkin' about, but I got me half a mind to punch your lights out!

MATTIE. Before or after you peel his banana?

FLORENCE. I've had just about enough of –

MATTIE. Call the sheriff, Greg dear! There's a payphone at the filling station up the street. Tell 'em to send a paddy wagon and an arrest warrant!

FLORENCE. On what charge?!

MATTIE. Let's not be coy. *(with growing Perry Mason-like intensity.)* Isn't it true, Mrs. Wexler, that you were bored with your husband, that you hated him, and took a young lover? Isn't it true that you purchased dynamite and rigged it to explode when Harry opened the door to the tool shed? Isn't it true that you concocted a phony story about flying saucers as an elaborate cover?

FLORENCE. Honey, you're about two beers short of a six pack! My husband is standing right here beside me, and if anyone's goin' to jail, it's you two for trespassing and disturbing the peace!

MATTIE. Madam, you're having visions. That is not Harold J. Wexler.

FLORENCE. I ain't havin' no vision, that's my husband! That! Right there! That's Harry!

MATTIE. *(totally confused)* …But-what…your-who-…your what…???

HUNK. *(mechanically)* This Earthling speaks the truth. I am Harold Wexler. Husband of Florence Wexler.

*(**FLORENCE** hits him, hard, His voice and demeanor change radically)*

I mean, how ya'll doin, nice tu meetcha, I'm Harry, wut's yur name?

FLORENCE. And as for you!!!! – *(some jolly whistling is heard, off)* OH good! Here comes Jack Primrose! *Sheriff* Jack Primrose, to be exact!

(SHERIFF JACK PRIMROSE enters. He is another strapping young hunk, rippling with muscles.)

MATTIE. Primrose?!?

SHERIFF PRIMROSE. *(mechanically, but not as bad as "Harry")* Evenin', Flo...Harry.

FLORENCE. Jack, honey, I'm so glad you was in the neighborhood.

SHERIFF PRIMROSE. Just makin' the rounds.

MATTIE. We were just going to call you, Sheriff. I'd like to report a murder!

SHERIFF PRIMROSE. There some kinda problem?

FLORENCE. I'll say there's a problem.

MATTIE. I'd say *murder* is a pretty damn big problem!

FLORENCE. These here are them two snoopy reporters everyone's been talkin 'bout –

MATTIE. Who's talking about us? We've only been in town two hours!

SHERIFF PRIMROSE. Lizard Lick ain't as big as New York City, Ma'am. News tends to travel pretty fast round these parts.

MATTIE. *(dryly:)* Does it, now?

SHERIFF PRIMROSE. Yes Ma'am, it does. Why my wife Dotty was just tellin' me ten minutes ago that –

GRAHAM. Excuse me, Sheriff...*Dotty*? Dotty Primrose, of the Evening Primrose Motor Lodge?

SHERIFF PRIMROSE. Well yes, you've met my wife, I take it?

MATTIE. Your *WIFE*?!?

GRAHAM. But Sheriff, that woman is old enough to be your grandmother!

MATTIE. Grandmother? That broad belongs in a wax museum! Why it's disgusting! Unnatural! Marriage is a union between a man and a woman of approximately the same age! What's going on in this town?

FLORENCE. I want these Yankees off my property, Jack.

MATTIE. It's supposed to be Adam and Eve, not Adam and Grandma Moses!

FLORENCE. If I were you, I'd throw 'em both in the drunk tank! They stink of whiskey...and cheap perfume.

MATTIE. This goddamn perfume ain't cheap!

SHERIFF PRIMROSE. We don't use language like that in Lizard Lick, Ma'am.

MATTIE. The hell you don't! Sewer mouth over here was screamin' "fuck mankind!"

FLORENCE. Why, I never used that evil word in my life!

MATTIE. What?! Tell him Gregory, you were here!

HARRY (THE HUNK). My wife don't lie, Jack.

GRAHAM. She certainly does lie, and she's not his wife!

SHERIFF PRIMROSE. *(handcuffing* **GRAHAM***)* All right, all right, I'm afraid I'm gonna hafta take you in.

GRAHAM. Hey now, what's the big idea?!? –

MATTIE. What the hell do you think you're doing?!?

GRAHAM. Ow! That hurts!

MATTIE. Unhand him, you hick bastard! We're Mattie Van Buren and Gregory Graham of *The New York Bugle*!

SHERIFF PRIMROSE. Miz Van Buren, I'm sorry but I –

MATTIE. On what charge are you arresting him, you sick pervert?!

SHERIFF PRIMROSE. Disorderly Conduct.

MATTIE. But he's not disorderly!

SHERIFF PRIMROSE. Preventive detention. Purely precautionary.

MATTIE. This is America. There's no such thing as preventive detention in America.

SHERIFF PRIMROSE. We make our own rules in Lizard Lick, Ma'am.

MATTIE. You will be sorry! You'll all be sorry! You don't know who you're dealing with!

HARRY. *(an ominous whisper)* Little lady, neither do you.

SHERIFF PRIMROSE. (*dragging* **GRAHAM** *off by the cuffs*) Bye now, Flo. Y'all take care –

GRAHAM. Mattie!

MATTIE. What are you doing?! Where are you going?! What about me?!

SHERIFF PRIMROSE. Miz Van Buren, we don't need you. The Silver Meteor's leaving in thirty-five minutes. Dotty's packed your bags. I suggest you go back to New York.

MATTIE. I'm not taking the train!

GRAHAM. Do as he says, Mattie! I can take care of myself!

MATTIE. Oh Gregory! Be brave, Gregory, dear! I'll get you outta that slammer if it takes me all night to do it!

SHERIFF PRIMROSE. (*as he exits with* **GRAHAM**) Now you stop figitin', Mr. Graham. This ain't gonna hurtcha a bit.

GRAHAM. Good-bye Mattie! I love you! I've always loved you!

MATTIE. Oh Gregory…….

(*They exit.* **MATTIE** *stares after them, horrified, her fist in her mouth.*)

FLORENCE. Girl, that's one man you ain't NEVER gonna see again.

MATTIE. (*distracted, only half heard her*) Wh-what did you say?

FLORENCE. (*brimming with smugness*) Nice to see ya again.

MATTIE. Ohh…oh yes of course.

FLORENCE. You take care a yourself, Miss Van Buren. And keep an eye out for them flyin' saucers.

MATTIE. (*still totally distracted, gazing off after* **GRAHAM**) Yes… yes of course. I'll do that…Good night, Mrs. Wexler… and Mr. Wexler…sorry to have troubled you…

FLORENCE. No trouble, honey…no trouble at all….

(*She lets out an evil little cackle and then exits inside. "*HARRY*" watches* **MATTIE** *for a moment and then turns to go back into the house, leaving* **MATTIE** *alone, center stage. Swoony sappy romantic music up.*)

MATTIE. He loves me…he's always loved me…but he's gone…oh so gone….and I…left oh so alone…

SONG – "SENSITIVE GIRL"

(She sings.)

I'M JUST A SENSITIVE GIRL
DEEP DOWN A SENSITIVE GIRL
WHO GAVE HER HEART TO HER WORK
PUSHED EVERYTHING ELSE AWAY

BUT THEN A HANDSOME YOUNG MAN
BEWITCHED THIS SENSITIVE GIRL
AND FOR A MOMENT OR THREE
SHE DREAMED MAYBE HE MIGHT STAY

BUT NOW HE'S GONE, GONE, GONE!
I AM ALL ALONE AGAIN AND I DONT KNOW WHAT TO DO
HE IS GONE, GONE, GONE!
AND MY JE NE SAIS QUOI AND MY CONFIDENCE ARE TOO
ALL I KNEW IS GONE, GONE, GONE, GONE!

(FLORENCE and "HARRY" slow dance in from stage right. MATTIE sees this and is horrified. She turns, just as DOTTY and "JACK PRIMROSE" slow dance on from stage left. It is too much for MATTIE, and she turns and slowly crosses downstage as the two romantic couples disappear into the mist. MATTIE sings.)

I'M JUST A SENSITIVE GIRL
A SCARED AND VULNERABLE GIRL.
BUT THOUGH THE WORLD'S GONE BERSERK
I'VE STILL GOT MY WORK TO DO.

I KNOW THIS PASSIONATE GIRL
SHE'LL FIND A WAY TO PULL THROUGH.
I AM A STRONG
BUT STILL A SENSITIVE GIRL.

(Then, we hear the sound of a distant, otherworldly choir. MATTIE freezes like a deer caught in headlights. tip-toes carefully toward the sound.)

MATTIE. That sound!....Who's there?!?...Who's out there??? I'm warnin' ya, I-I'm armed and dangerous!

(SHERIFF PRIMROSE enters upstage of her. He is texting on an electronic device while a bright colored light flashes in his ear. She turns with a start)

MATTIE. Oh, Sheriff Primrose. You scared me half to death. Did you hear that crazy choir? Why's you're ear flashing? What's that Dick Tracy gadget in your hand? Wait a minute! You're not Sheriff Primrose! You're not any kind of a sheriff.

(She turns to run as **HARRY WEXLER** *appears on the other side of the stage. He too is texting with an electronic device and has a flashing colored light in his ear.)*

MATTIE. Holy macaroni! You're sure as hell not Harry Wexler! You're not like us. You're…devil boys! Aliens! Put your weapons down. *(She pulls a small gun from her purse.)* Stop right there! I said put 'em down. I'm warning you!

(She shoots them both. They fall dead. **MATTIE** *faces front and screams a blood-curdling scream before she takes off running.)*

(quick blackout)

Scene Six

(Spotlight up on **MATTIE** *at a payphone.)*

MATTIE. Long distance, please. New York. Murray Hill three, two nine hundred. Tell 'em to reverse the charges, it's Mattie Van Buren. *Bugle?* Gimme Gil Wiatt. Quick! Gil? Don't you ever say that Mattie Van Buren won't eat crow. You were right. This place is crawling with aliens. I just shot two of them in the face. They're everywhere! Say listen, I got the whole story for you and it's a pip! The edition gone in yet? Good. Here's your headline: Devil Boys from Beyond Invade Florida! Entire Nation at Peril! *(busy signal)* Damn! Operator! Operator! I lost my connection!

(Blackout on **MATTIE***, lights up on* **WIATT** *on his office phone.)*

WIATT. Mattie! Mattie! Goddammit, I lost my connection. Velma! Call the pressroom. Tell 'em to rip open the bulldog and wait till they hear from me. Then get me the copy desk. And call Eastern Airlines. Book me on the next puddle jumper to Lizard Lick.

(Phone rings.)

WIATT. Wiatt here. Oh, McMahon, work your magic on this. "Terror strikes Eastern Seaboard. Untold thousands of alien creatures" – what did she call 'em? – "Devil boys invade from outer space. Panic in the streets! Call in the Marines! Nightmare on Elm Street!" You know how to make this work. *(He hangs up.)* I wonder what's really going on down there.

(blackout)

Scene Seven

(Florence Wexler's kitchen)

(A frantic rapping at the door.)

(FLORENCE enters with a ridiculously large rifle, aims it at the door. She is pregnant.)

FLORENCE. *(pleasantly enough)* Come on in and meet your maker…..!

(DOTTY PRIMROSE enters, wearing a long terry bathrobe, a kerchief and big slippers. She is pregnant.)

DOTTY. Florence, I've had a vision! A vision of doom! My eyeballs are burning like fire! Is it dark in here? …Are you pointing a gun at me?!

FLORENCE. Dotty, I'm just bearin my arms. The constitution says I can!

DOTTY. What in the world's gotten into you, honey?

FLORENCE. What's gotten into me? Why just about a dozen fat inches of alien love, baby!

DOTTY. Something's gone wrong with my eyes cause I swear you're nine months pregnant!

FLORENCE. And you ain't??????

DOTTY. *(nervous, scattered)* Pregnant? Me? Of course I ain't pregnant, just retainin' a little water's all!

FLORENCE. Whatcha retainin' there, honey, Lake Erie?

DOTTY. It's God's righteous punishment for my sin! We're all sinners!

FLORENCE. Talk all you like, Dotty Primrose, I feel like a brand new woman.

DOTTY. Well, ya look like a three dollar whore, and if we older women set a better example we might not draw so much attention to ourselves! I come over here to tell you the jig is up. Our goose is cooked!

FLORENCE. Dotty, you are one hell of a killjoy. What's eatin' you?

DOTTY. That lady reporter, Miz Van Buren, has been placing long distance calls to New York City. She's onto us.

FLORENCE. Them reporters have been dealt with, sister woman, you readin' me?

DOTTY. Florence, we have to repent, it's our only chance!

FLORENCE. Oh, loosen up, would ya? It's a miracle, what's happened to us, a miracle from God.

DOTTY. Well whatever it is, I'm havin' second thoughts about the whole damn thing.

FLORENCE. *(waves the gun at her menacingly)* I'm warnin' you, Dotty Primrose, if you do anything to screw this up for us, I'll fill you so fulla lead you'll shit pencils!

DOTTY. Florence honey, I just think –

FLORENCE. I don't care what you think! My bed ain't seen this much action since Harry brought home that Great Dane.

(DOTTY stares at her. A pause.)

Um, what I mean to say's you just mind your business!! *(suddenly turns sickly-sweet)* Now how 'bout a nice plate a fried eggs and griddle cakes.

DOTTY. Listen, I gotta run, Florence, I think I need to lie down a while.

FLORENCE. Good thinkin'. That baby needs all the rest it can get.

DOTTY. It ain't no baby, Florence Wexler, the whole damn thing's impossible.

FLORENCE. Oh, wake up and smell the alien invasion, Dotty! You've got a little green bun in the oven!

DOTTY. I felt a kick! It's kicking me! It wants out. We've got to repent! *(She exits.)*

FLORENCE. *(calls after her:)* NICE TALKIN' TO YA DOTTY! SEE YA IN THE DELIVERY ROOM!

(She cackles with great evil.)

(blackout)

(lights up quickly on:)

Scene Eight

(The Evening Primrose Motor Lodge)

(Mattie's and Gregory's room)

(MATTIE's hands shake as she pours herself a shot of whiskey. Knock at the door.)

MATTIE. Nooo....! No.........!!! Leave me alone!

WIATT'S VOICE. Let me in you crazy broad!

MATTIE. Gil! *(She lets him in)* Oh, I'm so glad you're here, thank God. How did you get here? How did you find me?

WIATT. I took the night flight from Idlewild. This is the only hotel in town. I figured you'd be here. I checked the registration book, and sure enough there was your name.

MATTIE. Oh Gil, you're good.

WIATT. Where's Graham?

MATTIE *(close to tears)* They've got him. They've got him.

WIATT. Well, then he's done for.

MATTIE. Done for?

WIATT. You heard me, honey! You think these alien bastards dropped in for a sun tan?!?

(There is a wild rapping at the front door.)

MATTIE. Oh, Gil, it's them, what do we do?!?

WIATT. Quiet you! I'll handle this!

LUCINDA'S VOICE. Gregory! Gregory, darling! Are you there?

WIATT. Who the hell is that?

MATTIE. *(goes to the door)* Oh, it's a creature all right, but not the kind that flies in saucers!

(She swings the door open. There stands LUCINDA, an absolute wreck. She wears dark glasses and a long, heavy trench coat. She is pregnant.)

LUCINDA. Mattie, dear, have you got a bromo? It's an absolute emergency. I have a terrible tummy ache. Where's Gregory?

MATTIE. He's gone! They got him! They got him! Oh Gilbert, I'm so scared!

LUCINDA. Gilbert! Whatever are *you* doing here?!

WIATT. I should ask the same, baby.

LUCINDA. *(thinking fast)* My interview was canceled. Audrey Hepburn was run over by a garbage truck.

MATTIE. Gil, ya know damned well this crone is lyin' through her crooked teeth!

WIATT. Dammit! Do you dames not get it?!? Alien creatures from the planet Pluto have invaded Lizard Lick! Their vile plan is to wipe every man, woman and child off the face of the Earth!

MATTIE. The planet Pluto? How do you know that?

WIATT. I'm just guessing. It's what we ran in the bulldog edition.

MATTIE. Plutopians, eh?! You may be on to something.

WIATT. Really? What the hell do *you* know about Pluto?!

MATTIE. Perhaps you've forgotten my father, Gil. The late great Professor Vladimir Stalinichky Von Buren.

LUCINDA. Of all the rubbish. The world-famous astronomer was *your* father??

WIATT. She's tellin' the truth, Lucinda. You knew of him?

LUCINDA. I knew Professor Von Buren well. He had quite a telescope.

(LUCINDA becomes increasingly more disturbed through the following.)

MATTIE. Oh what a lovely childhood we had, and naturally, I was Daddy's little girl. I never knew my mother, but Daddy said that was just as well. She was evil! A ruthless, wicked woman without a soul, she got pregnant on purpose so Daddy would marry her, and when he refused, she birthed me in a ditch and abandoned me on Daddy's door-step! I ask you! What kind of woman would do a wretched thing like that?

LUCINDA. *(thrown off balance, confused)* Perhaps the woman was young and foolish. Perhaps Professor Von Buren took advantage of an impressionable sixteen year-old girl! Perhaps he toyed with her emotions, pretending to be enamored of her very being, when all the BASTARD REALLY WANTED WAS TO FEEL HOT YOUNG FLESH PULSATING AGAINST HIS WITHERED SKIN! She was abandoned, scorned, and used! Her heart grew black and cold and hard as she carried that fetal ball of bitchery in her womb for nine long months and the only choice the poor girl had was to give the baby back to its worthless father!!!

*(**MATTIE** and **WIATT** stare at her.)*

Well....of course that's only ONE scenario.

WIATT. What the hell does this have to do with the end of the world?!? Mattie, what do you know about these Plutopians!?!

MATTIE. Why, the whole thing makes perfectly marvelous sense. You see, Pluto is a dark and dismal little rock that wasn't even discovered until 1930. It's an absolutely desolate place, and –

WIATT. Just get to the point!

MATTIE. Daddy always said that if there was life on that rotten boulder, the Earth would never be safe.

LUCINDA. Foolish girl! How could anything live in such a barren wasteland as the one you describe?!

MATTIE. On the surface, nothing could live. It's too cold to support life of any kind. But Daddy always suspected there to be a thriving reptilian society hidden just below the surface. It was his theory that the Plutopians live in underground cities.

LUCINDA. That can't be proven.

MATTIE. It can't be disproven.

WIATT. Intelligent?

MATTIE. Highly! Why, these creatures would have been around for millions of years before our planet was even born! Yet as accomplished as they'd be, their home planet remains nothing but a black, overgrown asteroid and they'd be forced to navigate the stars, ever searching for a home!

WIATT. And now they think they've found it here on Earth!

LUCINDA. Damn the bastards! They'll never get away with this!

WIATT. They may have gotten away with it already! They've kidnapped every man in this town, replacing them with Plutopians!

MATTIE. Is that true?

WIATT. I don't know.

LUCINDA. Pure nonsense! Surely the women would cause a great stir had their husbands been replaced with space monsters!

WIATT. Not if the women were put into some sort of a trance! Perhaps they think these impostors actually *ARE* their husbands!

MATTIE. Or perhaps the women are in on the whole thing!

LUCINDA. Really Matilda, I hardly think –

MATTIE. Don't cha get it?! This backwoods burg was perfect for their evil alien plot! The men here were fat, old, beer bellied inbreds, with a collective IQ of thirteen. Those Plutopians come flyin' down and whisk em all away to Neverland, Not only do their deadbeat husbands up and disappear, they're replaced, each and every one of em, with hot young studs ya could lick like a lollipop! Are these broads gonna sing to the coppers, I ask ya? Hell no, cause instead they spend all day and all night with their legs pointed up at the ceilin' and their kitty-cats flappin' in the wind!

WIATT. But why? Why do the Plutopians want our women?!?

MATTIE. Sex! They want these women flat on their backs until each and every one of em is burstin with an alien baby!

LUCINDA. Pregnancy! Matilda, really, you're far off the mark.

MATTIE. Oh, I am, am I? And I guess you just swallowed a basketball last night!

LUCINDA. Foolish girl! Whatever do you mean?

MATTIE. She's pregnant, Gil! I'd stake my –

LUCINDA. I won't listen to another word, Gilbert! This ridiculous excuse for a reporter has finally gone too far!

WIATT. Well, ya do look a little, um, big there, Lucinda.

MATTIE. Big? I'm tellin ya, Gil, she's gonna spill her slimy brood all over the carpet any second!

LUCINDA. What the hell are you suggesting?

MATTIE. You know damned well what I'm suggesting! You fucked a Plutopian!

LUCINDA. *(crumbling)* WHAT?!? It's true! It must be true! It's the only explanation! Last night, in my room, I heard strange and unusual noises! I noticed that the alien baby was gone from its jar!

WIATT. What the hell were you doin' with that jar?!?

MATTIE. She's a dirty thief, Gil. And mother to be of pure evil!

LUCINDA. I have no memory of what happened. I woke up the next morning, the creature was gone, as was my beautiful girlish figure!!! Yes, mock and taunt me if you will, Matilda Von Buren! But know this now! I'm your own flesh and blood!

MATTIE. The dame's gone daft.

LUCINDA. I speak the truth! I'm your mother, Matilda!

MATTIE. *(screams in horror)* Noooo! Gil, this lying Plutopian fucker would say anything!

WIATT. Leave it to a couple a broads to turn an alien invasion into a chapter out of Peyton Place!

MATTIE. But Gil –!

WIATT. No buts! We need to work together and there's no time to waste! If our theories are true, that means Gregory Graham's life is in grave danger!

MATTIE. Oh, hurry, Gil! We've got to bust him out of that slammer!

WIATT. Let's get out of here you two! It may already be too late!

MATTIE. Oh Gregory! Hold on Gregory, dear! Help is on the way!

(blackout)

Scene Nine

(In front of the mothership.)

(A big silver ramp pushes onstage.)

*(**HARRY** and **SHERIFF PRIMROSE** enter. Each carries a baby in a bundle. They go up the ramp and exit into the ship. They are dressed in sexy space-suits.)*

MATTIE. There it is.

WIATT. Great Caesar's ghost!

LUCINDA. The mother of all mother ships.

MATTIE. Gregory's in that awful place. Oh, I hate to think of him in there. We've got to get him out.

WIATT. I've got a plan. *(to **LUCINDA**)* And *you're* going to lead us.

LUCINDA. I'm going to lead us – *in there?*

MATTIE. Courage, Lucinda.

LUCINDA. There's only one thing I want you folks to do.

WIATT. What's that?

LUCINDA. Go fuck yourselves.

WIATT. Good God, here they come!

*(**DOTTY** enters from the Spaceship, no longer pregnant.)*

MATTIE. Mrs. Primrose!

DOTTY. Attention, Yankees! You've got nothing to fear if you cooperate!

*(**FLORENCE WEXLER** enters, dressed as the Queen of the Universe – a wild get up, with giant hair like the Bride of Frankenstein, and an impossible shiny red outfit, a cross between a space traveler and a dominitrix – think "Magenta" at the end of* The Rocky Horror Show. *She is no longer pregnant.)*

MATTIE. *(horrified)* Mrs. Wexler!

FLORENCE. So! Ya'll thought ya were real clever, didn't cha?! You pushy New Yorkers make my skin crawl!

WIATT. Lady, I don't know who you are, but I'll see you hang for treason!

FLORENCE. Why I'm just shakin' in my booties, baby. Now before my boys shoot ya'll fulla laser beams, anyone got any prayers to say?!?

MATTIE. Mrs. Wexler, how could you?!

WIATT. Don't talk to her Mattie, she's a filthy traitor!

MATTIE. Have you no shame?! Have you no decency?!?

FLORENCE. I have been chosen by the Ambassadors of Pluto to rule as High Empress of New Plutopia – that's the new name for the Planet Earth. Dotty's going to be my executive secretary. And together we will bring our Earthling brothers and sisters crumbling to their knees! They shall embrace Plutopian law with open arms or be destroyed!!

DOTTIE. Florence and I have just given birth to a new generation of invaders.

FLORENCE. But no more babies for this ol' girl. That thing crawled its way out of my coolie like Bella Lugosi.

MATTIE. You sick bastards'll never get away with this!

LUCINDA. Speak for yourself, daughter, dearest.

MATTIE. Lucinda Marsh! Even you wouldn't stoop so low as to betray your own planet!

LUCINDA. Wouldn't I? *(to* **FLORENCE***:)* Free Gregory Graham and I'll join your revolution!

MATTIE. Lucinda!

WIATT. I'd rather be ground into sausage links than live under alien oppression!!

MATTIE. Sing it, brother!

LUCINDA. Release Gregory Graham to me! We shall bow to Plutopian rule!

FLORENCE. That's more like it!

WIATT. You're fired, Lucinda Marsh!

LUCINDA. No, Gil, dear, *you're* fired! The *Plutopian Bugle* shall get along just fine without you!

MATTIE. You'll burn in hell for this, you bitch!

(There is a huge flash of white light directly off stage, accompanied by loud otherworldly choir. **HARRY** *and* **SHERIFF PRIMROSE** *enter from the ship.)*

FLORENCE *(running for cover)* Tell me when it's over! Tell me when it's over!

HARRY. Our ship is ready for departure. But first we would like to address the planet earth.

MATTIE. I shot both of them! I left them for dead in the street!

SHERIFF. Our immune systems are far more powerful than yours. All flesh wounds are healed instantly.

WIATT. The United States Armed Forces will track you down like wild animals. You don't stand a chance!

HARRY. You have no power over us.

SHERIFF. And we have come in peace.

MATTIE. Well, I've got news for you! You're *disturbing* the peace!

WIATT. But why have you come?

SHERIFF. First I will introduce myself. My name is Tattoo. This is my lover, Gort. We have been happily married for ninety-seven of your years.

MATTIE *(astonished)* Oh, my goodness! They're tutti-fruiti!

GORT. All marriage on Pluto is what you earthlings might call "same-sex" marriage.

WIATT. But why?

TATTOO. It's a gay planet.

LUCINDA. Christ, now I've heard everything.

TATTOO. We do have a system, and it works.

GORT. We live in harmony and unlike Earth creatures we have no tolerance for stupidity, bigotry, homophobia, or internecine hostility. But reproduction is difficult. So every seventeen years we travel to the Planet Virginis to breed. The Virginians are very welcoming.

TATTOO. It's always a real nice vacation.

GORT. Our landing on Earth was accidental due to a malfunction of our galactic positioning system.

TATTOO. The universe grows smaller every day. And accidents do happen. We have no intention of harming anyone.

GORT. And we have agreed to pay for the damaged tiles.

MATTIE. But what happened to Harry Wexler? And the Sheriff? That's a little something we earthlings call murder!

WIATT. Yeah!

TATTOO. Harry Wexler threatened us irrationally when we damaged his tool shed, and then the large men of Lizard Lick came.

GORT. They taunted us and tried to beat us and stab us with pitch forks. Their eyes were full of hate. And we were forced to put them all in sleep pods.

TATTOO. We thought earth was a terrible place. But it got better. Mrs. Wexler wasn't angry at all. She was joyful. She expressed a desire to be the mother of our children.

(All stare at **FLORENCE.***)*

FLORENCE. What was I supposed to do? My Harry was gone! I was alone! Gort became my soul-mate. It was a love story. A tragic love story. Don't leave me Gort! Please don't leave me!

GORT. Harry has been safely returned to your home, Florence.

FLORENCE. Now *that's* tragic.

LUCINDA. You mean this bitch *isn't* going to be empress of the planet?

GORT. Florence likes to engage in fantasy play. Don't you, Florence?

FLORENCE. Yes. Otherwise it's hard for me to reach orgasm.

WIATT. But what about *your* husband, Mrs. Primrose?

DOTTIE. That night I was changing the sheets at the Motel and cleaning the nickels out of the Magic Fingers when I heard voices. I thought I was having another vision.

FLORENCE. They call her a visionary.

DOTTIE. I heard a loud explosion and then a beautiful choir, the most beautiful sound I ever heard. I looked out the window and there was a blinding light in

Florence's backyard. It pricked my eyeballs like needles – LIKE NEEDLES! I went running toward the light, and that's when I seen him. It was love like I never felt it before.

GORT. Tattoo made a very strong impression on Dottie.

*(The **ALIENS** chuckle knowingly.)*

TATTOO. And it wasn't long before she asked us to put Sheriff Primrose in a sleep pod too.

(They chuckle again.)

LUCINDA. That's all well and good, but what about the alien who impregnated me? I regret to say I didn't have such a great time.

GORT. *(to **LUCINDA**)* You?

TATTOO. *(to **GORT**)* Did you?

GORT. *(to **TATTOO**)* No, did you?

TATTOO. We don't know what you're talking about.

LUCINDA. That hideous green thing with the slimy tentacles.

TATTOO. Oh, we've been looking all over for him!

GORT. That's our pet, Pow-Pow. He can be a little aggressive.

TATTOO. Have you found him?

LUCINDA *(looking down at pregnant belly with disdain)* I think so.

WIATT. Well, I'll be a monkey's uncle!

MATTIE. I don't believe it! These women are too old to be pregnant!

TATTOO. These women that you call mothers of our offspring are not the parents. They were nurse to the seed, the new-sown seed that grew and swelled inside them. All Plutopians are a self-fertilizing source of life.

MATTIE. But where's Gregory?

TATTOO. He too is fine.

*(**GREGORY** enters down the ramp, runs to **MATTIE**.)*

GREGORY. *(embracing her)* Mattie!

MATTIE. Oh, Gregory, you're alive! I thought I'd never see you again! My darling, are you okay?

GREGORY. I feel ten years younger. Those sleep pods are terrific.

WIATT. Were you tortured?

GREGORY. Good heavens, no. Tattoo and Gort have been fantastic. And I've got exclusive photos of the private lives of the Plutopians.

WIATT. The *Bugle* is saved!

CROWD. Hooray!

GREGORY. What's more, I think I've kicked booze for good. Tattoo and Gort made me realize why I drank. Mattie, I'm a repressed homosexual. What's wrong, Mattie? Aren't you happy for me?

MATTIE. Of course I am. It's just that…I was hoping that we could be remarried one day.

GREGORY. We can be! We should be! Don't you see, I can't be openly homosexual, not on this planet. I'm going to need a cover. We could have the perfect marriage. You like to spend your evenings in the newsroom at the *Bugle*, I like to spend mine in the men's room at the New York Public Library. Mattie, would you be my beard?

MATTIE. That's a very generous offer, Greg. I'll have to think long and hard about it.

LUCINDA. I always knew you were a cocksucker, Graham. And I'm going to expose you in my column the minute we get back to little old New York.

WIATT. What are you saying, Lucinda? I can't run his photo essay if you tell the world he's a faggot!

LUCINDA *(hoisting a bottle from her purse)* The only running you're going to be doing is out of town on a rail, Wiatt. I'm exposing *you* as a communist. I'd like to propose a toast! Here's to all the pinkos, commies, queers, and fag hags in this fucked-up world – I bid you a fond farewell! *(She drinks.)*

(The **ALIENS** *are horrified.)*

TATTOO. *(attempting to wrest the bottle from her)* No, No!

GORT. You can't drink alcohol!

LUCINDA. Whaddaya mean I can't drink? I could drink you under the table you pathetic little queen.

(She drinks.)

TATTOO. It's too late.

GORT. Alcohol is deadly to Plutopians

LUCINDA *(writhing in agony)* What's happening to me?

(LUCINDA's pregnant stomach deflates, and smoke rises from it.)

My uterus! *(She collapses. A raspy moan.)* Matilda…come close…

GRAHAM. Don't do it Mattie, it's a dirty trick!

LUCINDA. …It's…no trick, Gregory, darling…I'm done for….

(LUCINDA is sprawled on the ground. MATTIE kneels to her.)

MATTIE. *(almost tenderly)* Oh, Lucinda, why? You destroyed my reputation, crushed my marriage, scooped my story, threatened to expose Gilbert as a communist and Greg as a fruitcake!

LUCINDA. I only wanted…to be loved…

MATTIE. But at what cost?!

LUCINDA. I was oh so wrong, I see that now. Oh, Matilda… Can you ever forgive me?

MATTIE. *(with great drama)* Mother.

LUCINDA. *(with her dying breath)* Daughter.

(LUCINDA dies.)

MATTIE. Oh, Gregory, how can it be true? Is she really….

GRAHAM. …She's dead, Mattie.

MATTIE. Oh, Gregory, I never thought…I never thought I'd live to see this moment! Lucinda Marsh is dead! It's a miracle from God!!

(She throws herself into GRAHAM's arms, weeping.)

GORT. We must leave your planet now. But I see that you're sad. It is possible that our medical technology could revive her

TATTOO. We would have to take her body back to Pluto.

MATTIE *(considers it for a moment)* Do it.

DOTTY. Tattoo! Don't go!

(**GORT** *and* **TATTOO** *pick up* **LUCINDA**'s *body and carry her into the Mother Ship.*)

FLORENCE. Whaddaya wanna do tonight, Dottie?

DOTTIE. I dunno. What do you wanna do tonight, Florence?

FLORENCE. I dunno. *My Little Margie*'s on at eight-thirty.

WIATT. Excuse me, ladies, but I have an offer to make. How would you like to be world-famous?

FLORENCE. What's in it for us?

WIATT. A trip to New York City.

DOTTIE. New York City's evil.

WIATT. Dancing at the Stork Club.

DOTTY. We don't need any more storks.

FLORENCE *(considering it)* Speak for yourself, Dotty. I'd like to kick up my heels.

MATTIE. Lay it on, Gil. The key to the city! Maybe even a ticker tape parade!

WIATT. You'll be on *Person to Person* with Ed Murrow, *Today* with Dave Garroway!

DOTTIE. We're gonna be on TV?

MATTIE. Wait a minute, you louse. Aren't you forgetting something? This is my story!

WIATT. And of course a front page story with Mattie Van Buren's byline and photos by Gregory Graham.

DOTTIE. Florence! We can form a vaudeville act!

FLORENCE. We could dance!

DOTTIE. Yes!

FLORENCE. We could sing!

DOTTIE. We could play the Palace!

FLORENCE. We'll call ourselves the Lizard Sisters.

DOTTIE. Let's go home and pack, Flo.

FLORENCE. I'm right behind ya, momma!

MATTIE. Doesn't anyone have the heart to tell them that vaudeville's dead?

WIATT. Never mind that. If we hurry we can still make the red eye outta here.

MATTIE. Oh, Gil…I'm not sure I can. What I mean is, you'll have to give the story to someone else. Gil, dear. I quit. For real this time.

Graham. What?!

WIATT. Hey, what's the big idea?

MATTIE. You two go on and make the old hags famous.

WIATT. Ya just said it was your story! And it is! And you'll win every award around!

MATTIE. Paper and gold, that's all. Paper and gold. They can't take the place of God's most precious gift. Life. And I realize now that I've spent my own life living a lie. In love with an unreachable man, and spending every minute of every day writing about others. No, Gil. It's time I hung up my hat and spent some time getting to know a very special person – Mattie Van Buren.

WIATT. Aw Mattie, you can't! The Bugle needs you!

GRAHAM. And you're the only writer I can work with! It's true, Mattie. I know that now.

MATTIE. Oh, Gregory, darling. It's too late.

GRAHAM. But what about us?

MATTIE. We could never have a true marriage.

GRAHAM. Is it because I'm…

MATTIE. No. I'll admit that when you told me you were homosexual I found it hard to swallow, but now I realize that I simply never knew you, and I could never be married to a stranger.

GRAHAM. Could I never be more than a stranger to you?

MATTIE. Perhaps. But it would take the greatest miracle of all.

GRAHAM. The greatest miracle. What's that?

MATTIE. You and I would both have to transform to the point that...

WIATT. Hey! They're taking off!

(There is a roar and the Mother Ship takes off. All run toward it, waving and shouting "Good-bye!")

MATTIE. You know, Greg, they were a little creepy, but they were nice fellas.

GREGORY. Maybe we could learn something from them.

WIATT. Let's go home, kids. I got a paper to get out.

(MATTIE and GREGORY laugh.)

(Blackout. Lights flash up on a photo tableau of FLOR-ENCE and DOTTY winking at the camera.)

The End

CUE: *Florence and Harry Exit*

Sensitive Girl
from Devil Boys from Beyond

Music & Lyrics by:
Drew Fornarola

Sensitive Girl

gone, gone, gone! I am all a-lone a-gain in the foul Flor-id-ian goo. He is

gone, gone, gone! and my... je ne sais quoi, and my con-fi-dence ___ are too. All I

(tracked high note, 8va)

knew is gone, gone (gone!) _____

Sensitive Girl

but though the world's gone ber-serk, I've still got my work to do.

I know this pas-sion-ate girl, she'll find a way to pull

through. I am a strong, but still a sensitive, girl.

poco rall.

PROPERTY PLOT

Scene One: Gil Wiatt's Office in the Newsroom
   Desk
   Intercom on desk
   Black telephone on desk
   2 Airline ticket envelopes on desk (Eastern Airlines)
   Itinerary on desk
   Alien baby in jar in drawer of desk
   2 Chairs

Scene Two: An Airliner
   5 Chairs
   Life Magazine (**MATTIE**)
   Newspaper (NY Bugle??) (**LUCINDA**)
   Small vanity case or large purse (**LUCINDA**)
   Small bourbon bottle or flask with liquid) (in suitcase)
   Shot glass (in suitcase)
   Alien baby puppet not in jar (in suitcase)
   Toy airplane on a stick

Scene Three: **MATTIE** and **GREGORY**'s Room at the Evening
Primrose Motel
   Chair
   Side table
   Luggage rack
   Suitcase (with dressing such as nightgowns, underwear, etc.)
   Bourbon bottle (inside suitcase)
   Funnel (inside suitcase)
   Camera with flash (**GREGORY**)
   Large alien puppet at window

Scene Four: **LUCINDA**'s Room at the Evening Primrose Motel
   Chair
   Side Table
   Luggage rack with Lucinda's suitcase
   Jar of cold cream (**LUCINDA**)
   2 bottles of bourbon (in **LUCINDA**'s suitcase)
   Alien baby in jar rigged to pop out

Scene Five: **FLORENCE WEXLER**'s Porch
   Handcuffs—practical (**SHERIFF**)
   Press ID (**MATTIE**)
   2 electronic devices (**SHERIFF** and **HARRY**)
   2 flashing earpieces (**SHERIFF** and **HARRY**)
   Blank pistol—practical (**MATTIE**)

Scene Six: Split Scene—Lizard Lick Payphone and Newsroom
    Pay telephone receiver (**MATTIE**)
    Desk phone receiver (**GIL**)

Scene Seven: **FLORENCE WEXLER**'s Kitchen
    Large rifle (**FLORENCE**)

Scene Eight: **MATTIE** and **GREGORY**'s Motel Room
    Chair
    Side table
    Whisky bottle (**MATTIE**)
    Shot glass (**MATTIE**)
    Blank pistol, same as Scene Six (**MATTIE**)

Scene Nine: The Bog near the Space Ship
    Door to space ship
    Entry path to space ship (rope lights)
    2 baby bundles (**ALIENS**)
    Liquor flask (**LUCINDA**)
    Tip of Space Ship (offstage)

A NOTE ABOUT
THE PRODUCTION

Devil Boys from Beyond is a loving parody of classic and not-so-classic films from a variety of genres, such as 1950s sci-fi (*Invasion of the Body Snatchers, The Day the Earth Stood Still, Invaders from Mars*), hardboiled newspaper comedy (*The Front Page, His Girl Friday, It Happened One Night*), and conventional melodrama (*The Lost Weekend, The Strange Loves of Martha Ivers*). Add a touch of Tennessee Williams and turn on the blender!

While there is certainly room for outrageous clowning, the play works best when the world of these films is accurately recreated on stage. Actors should be encouraged to research their roles by viewing some of these vintage films in order to understand the heightened style of the period. It is often more effective to play it straight than to "ask" for the laugh with excessive mugging. The original cast was all male, but the play could be easily and effectively played with a mix of men and women.

The circumstances of the New York International Fringe Festival necessitated that the scenic design of the original production of *Devil Boys from Beyond* be kept extremely simple. We shared the theatre with many other productions, and we were allotted fifteen minutes to assemble the set before the house opened, and fifteen minutes to put everything away after the curtain call. Our set designer, B.T. Whitehill, came up with a stylish, abstract backdrop that suggested the time period and the subject matter. All the scenes were played in front of this backdrop, and changes in location were accomplished with lighting and a few simple scenic elements that were easily moved on and off by the actors and our "Newsboys." This approach worked well because it allowed for swift transitions from scene to scene.

(From left to right:)
Jacques Mitchell as Sheriff Jack Primrose/Tattoo; Andy Halliday as Dotty Primrose; Jeff Riberty as Harry Wexler/Gort; Everett Quinton as Florence Wexler; Robert Berliner as Gregory Graham; Paul Pecorino as Mattie Van Buren; Peter Cormican as Gilbert Watt; Chris Dell'Arno as Lucinda Marsh

Photo by B.T. Whitehill

Also by
Buddy Thomas...

The Crumple Zone

Physical

Spotlight

Please visit our website **samuelfrench.com** for complete descriptions and licensing information

OTHER TITLES AVAILABLE FROM SAMUEL FRENCH

THE CRUMPLE ZONE

Buddy Thomas

Comedy / 5m / Interior

This hilarious off Broadway hit, set in a run down apartment on Staten Island, concerns three gay roommates coming to crisis during one frantic Christmas weekend. Terry, an out of work actor who can't keep a job or get a date, spends his days swilling cheap vodka and playing referee to a messy love triangle. Extremely funny and deeply moving, *THE CRUMPLE ZONE* is about staying together, breaking apart and the things we lose along the way.

"The kind of domestic comedy that might have been written by Neil Simon if he were gay and 40 years younger!"
– *The New York Times*

"A little gem."
– Liz Smith

"Guaranteed to keep the laughter in overdrive!"
– *New York Daily News*

"Sparkles! The first fresh comedy of its type to come along in years. It is not going too far to draw parallels between Neil Simon or Kaufman & Hart at the top of their powers.... A rollicking farce with a heart of pure gold."
– *LGNY Newspaper.*

OTHER TITLES AVAILABLE FROM SAMUEL FRENCH

PHYSICAL

Buddy Thomas

Comedy / 2m, 2f / Interioe

It is the coldest night in November. Owen has shelved his college books and thesis papers to prepare for the date of his life. With candlelight, soft music and enough Italian chicken to feed the Northeast coast, he is ready but not for Aurora, the drugstore cosmetics cashier he has finally had the courage to ask for a date. All lipstick and hair spray and spike heels, Aurora is a combination of every cover girl in the history of Cosmopolitan, but her brain is made of paper too. Nothing goes as planned. When Aurora falls for Owen's roommate, things really get out of hand. Throw in Frieda, a psycho obsessive neighbor who has weddings with Barbie dolls and wields a mean butcher knife, and you have a physical comedy of lunatic proportions. Note: Includes numerous great monologues and scenes.

OTHER TITLES AVAILABLE FROM SAMUEL FRENCH

SPOTLIGHT

Buddy Thomas

Comedy / 2m, 2f / Unit Set

From the author of the hit plays *Devil Boys From Beyond* and *The Crumple Zone* comes this hilarious one-act about college theatre majors waiting for the cast list for *West Side Story* to be posted.....and the aftermath. A finalist in HBO's New Writer's Workshop and a Second Place winner at American College Theatre Festival, Spotlight is a fast-paced comedy about the desperate drive to succeed, and delusions that get in the way.

OTHER TITLES AVAILABLE FROM SAMUEL FRENCH

VAMPIRE LESBIANS OF SODOM

Charles Busch

Adventurous Groups

Farce / 6m, 2f / Unit Set

This truly bizarre entertainment of the *Rocky Horror* genre is about vamps, has nothing to do with lesbians and takes the audience from ancient Sodom to the Hollywood of the twenties and ends up in present day Las Vegas.

"Costumes flashier than pinball machines, outrageous lines, awful puns, sinister innocence, harmless depravity - it's all here. One can imagine a cult forming."
– *The New York Times*

"Bizarre and wonderful...If you think Boy George is a gender-bender, well, like Jolson said, you ain't seen nothing yet! Forget your genders, come on, get happy."
– *Broadway Magazine*